First Book of
TRACTORS
AND FARM VEHICLES

Jean Coppendale

QED Publishing

Copyright © QED Publishing 2007

First published in the UK in 2007 by
QED Publishing
A Quarto Group company
226 City Road
London EC1V 2TT

www.qed-publishing.co.uk

A Catalogue record for this book is available from the British Library.

ISBN 978 1 84538 641 2

Written by Jean Coppendale
Designed by Joita Das (Q2A Media)
Editor Katie Bainbridge
Picture Researcher Jyoti Sachdev (Q2A Media)

Publisher Steve Evans
Creative Director Zeta Davies
Senior Editor Hannah Ray

Printed and bound in China

Picture credits

Key: t = top, b = bottom, c = centre,
l = left, r = right, FC = front cover
CLAAS KGaA ltd: 5t; Dave Reede/**AGStockUSA:** 6-7;
Mirek Weichsel/**AGStockUSA:** 10-11;
Index Stock Imagery/ Photolibrary: 10b;
Agripictures: 13t; Dave Reede/**AGStockUSA:** 14-15;
Holt Studios: 15t; **CLAAS:** 16-17;
New Holland: 18-19; **Valtra:** 20-21

Words in **bold** can be found
in the glossary on page 23.

Contents

What is a tractor? **4**

Watch those wheels! **6**

Preparing the fields **8**

Sowing the seeds **10**

Looking after the crops **12**

Harvest time...................................... **14**

Collecting wheat................................ **16**

Baling straw...................................... **18**

Pull, tractor! **20**

Activities **22**

Glossary **23**

Index... **24**

What is a **tractor?**

cab

The driver's cab is almost all glass so the driver can see what is happening around him.

This tractor is pulling a heavy trailer across a field.

Tractors are big machines that are used mainly on farms. They help farmers to prepare their land, plant and care for their crops, and **harvest** them when they are ready.

A tractor has a **cab** where the driver sits. Other machines can be hooked onto the back of the tractor so it can do lots of different jobs.

Watch those wheels!

A tractor has big wheels so that it can travel across rocky, bumpy fields. The huge wheels help to stop the tractor from sinking into muddy ground.

Very heavy tractors have double wheels and some even have three wheels on either side.

The wheels are specially made so that they can grip soft, muddy earth.

Preparing the fields

Farmers need to prepare their fields before they can plant **crops**. To do this the farmer attaches a **plough** to the back of the tractor.

A plough is a long row of metal blades. The blades turn as they are pulled through the earth.

The plough has sharp **blades** that cut through the soil. As the tractor pulls the plough through the fields, the blades chop up the soil and turn it over, leaving rows of ditches or **furrows**.

Sowing the seeds

When the fields are ready, farmers plant, or sow, the seeds. They do this with a seed drill. The seed drill is a container, or row of containers, that is attached to the back of the tractor. The containers are filled with seeds.

This seed drill is being filled with corn seeds.

As the seed drill is pulled across the fields, seeds travel from the containers down lots of little pipes that drop them into the furrows in the ground.

The seed drill plants the seeds in straight rows.

Looking after the crops

Once they start growing, the new crops need to be looked after. Some farmers spray their fields with a special liquid which stops insects from eating the crops and stops weeds from growing.

Some farmers do not use sprays on their crops. Instead, workers pull up the weeds by hand as they are pulled through the fields.

A machine called a crop sprayer is attached to the back of a tractor. As the tractor moves through the fields, the liquid is sprayed through pipes onto the growing crops.

The crop sprayer has long arms at either side which spray the crops.

Harvest time

When the farmer's crops are fully grown, it is time to harvest them. Lots of machines are used to harvest different crops. Vegetable harvesters dig up vegetables which grow under the ground.

The green tractor is pulling a machine that harvests potatoes.

The vegetable harvester pulls the vegetables out of the ground and drops them into a truck that is driven next to the tractor.

Some harvesters can pull up two rows of carrots at a time.

Collecting wheat

Wheat is ready to harvest when it is tall and **ripe**. This is done with a machine called a combine harvester. The machine at the front of the harvester has sharp blades that spin around.

In very big fields many combine harvesters work together.

As the blades of the machine spin, they cut the long stalks of wheat.

The wheat is then sucked into the harvester where the **grain** is separated from the stalk.

Baling straw

After a field of wheat has been harvested, the cut stalks are left behind – this is called straw. A special machine called a baler cuts the straw and makes it into round or square **bales**.

The bales of straw are tied up tightly and dropped out of the baler.

New Holland
BR560

A tractor loads the bales of straw onto a trailer and takes them away to be stored.

The straw is used as food for farm animals. During the winter, straw is also used as bedding for the animals.

Pull, tractor!

Some tractors can be used
for fun as well as for work.
Tractor races are very
noisy and exciting.
People watch to
find out which
tractor can pull
the heaviest weight.

These tractors have huge back wheels to stop them from slipping. The tractors race along a special **track** pulling a heavy load behind them while the crowd shouts and cheers.

During a race, the front wheels may lift off the ground completely.

Activities

- Would you like to be a farmer driving a big tractor? Would it be fun? Would it be hard work? Draw a picture of yourself driving a tractor.

- Here are two tractors you have seen in the book. Can you remember what jobs they do?

- Write a story about a runaway tractor. How will your story start? Who will be in your story? What happens at the end? Can you draw a picture to go with your story?

- Look through the book again. Write a list of jobs that are done on the farm and the machines you would need to do them. How many different machines do you need? Which do you think would be your favourite job? Why?

Glossary

Bales
Large bundles of cut hay or straw that are tied up very tightly.

Blades
Sharp, flat pieces of metal used for cutting. The flat, sharp metal part of a knife is called a blade.

Cab
A place on top of the tractor where the driver sits and uses the controls for moving the tractor.

Crops
Any plants that the farmer grows, such as vegetables or wheat.

Furrows
Long, narrow cuts in the ground made by a plough.

Grain
The part of the wheat that is used to make flour for bread. Grains are like tiny seeds.

Harvest
To cut and collect together all the crops that are fully grown or ripe.

Plough
A machine that breaks up the soil and prepares it for the seeds to be planted.

Ripe
When crops are fully grown and are ready to harvest.

Track
A special pathway where tractors race.

Index

activities 22

animals 19

baler 18

bales 18, 23

baling straw 18-19

blades 8, 9, 16, 17, 23

cab 4, 5, 23

carrot harvester 15

combine harvester 16-17

crop sprayer 13

crops 5, 8, 12-13, 23

driver 4, 5

farms 5, 23

fields 8-9

furrows 9, 11, 23

grain 17, 23

harvest 5, 14-17, 23

insects 12

plough 8-9, 23

potato harvester 14-15

preparing fields 5, 8-9

pulling weights 20-21

races 20-21

ripe 16, 23

seed drill 10-11

sowing seeds 10-11

sprays 12, 13

straw 18-19

track 21, 23

tractor races 20-21

trailers 5

vegetable harvesters
    14-15

weeds 12, 13

wheat 16-17, 18

wheels 6-7, 21